For Michelle and Catherine - S.V.
For Jessie Bambridge - J.D.

First published in Great Britain in 1994 by Andersen Press Ltd., 20 Vauxhall Bridge Road, London SW1V
2SA. Published in Australia by Random House Australia Pty., 20 Alfred Street, Milsons Point, Sydney,
NSW 2061. All rights reserved. Colour separated in Switzerland by Photolitho AG, Offsetreproduktionen,
Gossau, Zurich. Printed and bound in Italy by Grafiche AZ, Verona.

10 9 8 7 6 5 4 3 2 1

British Library Cataloguing in Publication Data available.

ISBN 0 86264 455 0

This book has been printed on acid-free paper

The SPRING RABBIT

Written by JOYCE DUNBAR

Illustrated by SUSAN VARLEY

Andersen Press · London

ALL the little rabbits that lived in the wood had brothers and sisters. All except Smudge.

"Why haven't I got a sister or a brother?" he asked his mother.

"Wait until the spring," she answered.

SPRING seemed a long way away.

Smudge watched on a cold autumn morning as the other rabbits chased falling leaves. Then he had an idea. He made a leaf rabbit with leafy broken twigs.

"You can be my brother," he said to the leaf rabbit. "Let's chase each other down the hill."

The leaf rabbit didn't answer.

THEN the wind blew all the leaves away,
leaving only the bare twigs.
"Wait until the spring," said a mouse.

B<small>UT</small> spring was a long time coming.
   Later, the snow fell. Smudge made a snow rabbit.
"You can be my sister," he said to the snow rabbit. "Let's
have a game of snowball."
   But the snow rabbit couldn't play snowball.

N EXT day, the snow rabbit melted.
"Wait until spring," said a robin.

B UT spring was a long time coming.
  When the snow melted, Smudge made a mud rabbit.
"You can be my brother," he said to the mud rabbit.
"Let's splash about in the puddles."

B<small>UT</small> the mud rabbit didn't splash about.
The rain came and washed it away.
"Wait until spring," said a frog.

A T LAST came the first signs of spring. All the twigs were sprouting green shoots and the buds were beginning to show.

Smudge went looking for his brother. He looked in the hollows of the trees, but he found no sign of a brother, only a mouse hole, full of baby mice.

"There are no rabbits here," said the mouse.

HE LOOKED in the bushes and brambles, but he didn't find a brother there either, only a bird's nest, with six speckled eggs.

"There are no rabbits here," said the robin.

HE LOOKED in the reeds by the pond, but he didn't find a
brother there either, only frogspawn full of tiny tadpoles.

"There are no rabbits here," said the frog.

Smudge felt very sad and lonely. At last he went home.

"I CAN'T find my spring brother anywhere," he said to his mother.

"You were looking in all the wrong places," she said, showing him three tiny bundles. "See what we have here."

Smudge was overjoyed. He had two baby brothers and a sister. As soon as they were hopping about he made them an enormous moss rabbit . . .

. . . and everyone knew that spring had come.